U

A book of

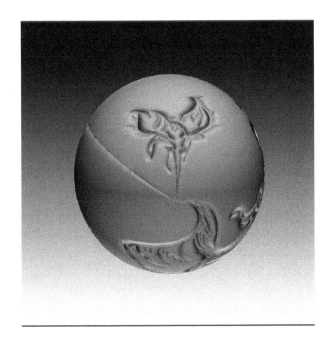

Author:
Bernard Frank

Under a Canopy of Trees... A Book of poetry, images and
self-expression
Unabridged edition Copyright March 2021, Frank
Bernard Johnson, all rights reserved.
Published By: Frank Bernard Johnson
ISBN 978-1-716-87683-7

Authored *by* Bernard Frank
Edited *by* Bernard Frank

9 781716 876837

PREFACE

A lot of times people will sit down and write these depressing diatribes of abject human misery in order to invoke an emotional response. This is usually allowed to pass for poetry. Some feet of literature that is (*read again with sarcasm*). It's like picking at an old scab until it bleeds and the proclaiming yourself a surgeon. Touch an emotion more heavily guarded and maybe there will be some merit to the claim of literary genius.

Shakespeare, the brothers Grimm: now there are some individuals who brought poetry to life by tapping emotions that are not so publicly displayed. Shakespeare has made us laugh and feel the butterflies in our stomach that we call first love. The brothers Grimm put fear and horror in our hearts during a time when showing fear could lead to the assassination of nobles.

Grab your reader from the inside. Wrath and suffering are the emotional billboards in our society. Aggression and defeat are how we measure our own progress as well as others. Everyone wants to show their aggressive side because we equate it with strength. We readily show our defeats because it builds a sense of community. Conversely, love and fear are subjective and individual, and can only show weakness.

People choose to be aggressive, and they admit defeat. Love carries us away and fear paralyzes us. These emotions can control us. Poets, honest and true, can also write in such a way that their words make the reader feel contrary to what they choose. The reader feels the way the poet wishes them to feel even though the reader prefers to feel otherwise.

強度

Why Sometimes I Look at You in Silence

There are two of us.
Gasping, clawing, churning, burning,
Whispering that engine to sleep.
Smokestacks of emotion
Gushing, billowing, bumbling, fumbling.
The swelling inside that diminishes our individual
significance.
*   *   *

Squishing, melding, crashing, crunching,
In a whirlpool that drains the sky.
Grinding, spinning, sloshing, sloppily
Butterfly emotions float the Walls of Jericho to the ground.
Each new day the Sun romps, thunders, trounces and
pounces above our earth.
*   *   *

My eyes are left in a deluge, red wrinkled and worn
As cries from joys long gone dissipate into the past.
Yesterdays fade into tomorrow, blurred by the brightness of
today.
Clutched by an eternal fear, I imagine I speak the words
but leave them unsaid.
I... you

One Day Off

I think I would enjoy beginning most days sitting on my porch watching the shadows grow shorter. Smelling the scent of nature's trees and morning dew. Watching it all slowly morph into streams of asphalt and towers of steel.

Ever shorter the shadows would grow as the sun lumbers across the sky, illuminating the day laborers in its spotlight. Their haunches beading with a golden sweat that will be later pooled into futures offering plate.

The shadows will eventually grow long again but twist differently from the days. Misshaped and thinned under an army of incandescent and florescent lights- gnarled figures crouched under desk lamps.

I think it would be nice to end most days sitting on my porch watching steel night birds fly flapless. Listening to cars blow through the wind, while silent twinkles are echoed in the concrete trees. Watching towers grow taller under the reduced weight of night shift.

A low moan from the nocturnal worker bee would hum me to sleep, as its songs signifies the start of a new night. A night of sowing fresh seeds for the morrow.

A Letter to My...

My passion swells for you like the mighty sea.
Massive and unyielding, it
Malays under its own weight
Crashing forward overlapping, spilling.
Each drop warmed and cooled by your love of me.

Is it Over Yet?

Time

That crushing weight that bows men's spirit is equal to that of the sun. Its power derived from simple persistence, nurtured by a cutting longevity. I ply my patients into a shield. A shiny trinket to distract my mind. But steady and on course is she.

Time.

It is not mine, nor yours or any coalitions, she is self-emanating. Whether I perceive her as constant or in short intervals- she decides. And should I not perceive her I am cast aside. Replaced with another perceive-her. Dancing haplessly from life to life price tagging each with duration.

Time.

Periods and intervals contingent on moments lead and follow by their asses. If turned in reverse time stays as she passes. Chasing an ever-birthing fantasy called the End.

Three Times. Four Lines. One Passion

You dole out portions of passion.
Passed out like hors d'oeuvres.
Merely enough to taste not to fill,
Bringing me to beg like hungry a feline at your feet.

Desire's aroma falls out of fashion
Without the respect our sex deserves.
The medicine toughest to hate, makes you ill.
Savoring a tart realty with hints of delusions sweet.

Marked and, marred...
Mourned becomes our unanswered hope.
Coveted as a savior, passion offers no solace.
Benign she seems, collapsing then resurrecting herself.

Yearning, yawing, yoking.
Obeying impulses to cope.
Building our prison, painting it as a palace,
Her wilting is a deception, she is evolving in stealth.

Don't Look Up.

In a wishing well sky there is no top.
The center of nights cool dark sky is a jar of bell.
Brightly it glimmers and we follow like moths.

The freckled night is unassuming and easy to view; we
cannot stop.
Its patterned visage swirls imaginations, our infant's view
from inside our shell.
The great empty as it is known, holding the only lights we
can't turn off.

Square Peg Round Hole

It's sad that we wish so hard.
Pit our hope against the hopelessness,
Spiting the world, wanting our prayers answered before the
lot.

Square pegs begging to fit in round holes.
Sinners knowing kneeling will never a save their soul.
Scrambling for the ears of our adjudicator, all for not.

Rubbing rabbits feet.
Clicking our heels three times,
Abandoning reason, because it leaves us dammed.

Cross hatching lies into truths.
Knotting off our past to make knew roots.
Roots at the core of our beginning, all tightly crammed.

So we smudge the truth, change perspective in hindsight's
view.
Washing time's window, streaking the pain with wishful
thinking, hope, and unspoken regret.
But the truth never changes on the other side of that
window.... At least not yet.

Where the Grass Grows Short,
And the Shadows Long

Far and away in a land that I can't find on any map, you
reside. Hot, jaded
and bare naked, to the world you show your hand.

It's never exactly cold there, though at times there is a bit of
a chill. A brief reprieve not lasting long enough to forget
that overbearing heat.

Heat with the sun. Heat with the moon. Always an
unyielding simmering that brings you to a slow roast.
I hope you're happy in this land where you sit day after day
alone. I hope you're happy there and that you never leave...

Fallen

This beautiful Heart.
This beautiful Mind.
This beautiful Soul.
This beautiful Person.

How deeply I have fallen in love with this person.

I pray to God I continue to fall.
That we fall together.
That we never reach the bottom.

The Empty Space is Now Full

Paddling, Panting Processing.
Routing, Running, Rating.
Watching, Waiting, Working.

Grinding, Gathering, Giving.
Longing, Loving, Learning.
Kneading, Kneeling Knuckling.

Sparring, Sparing, Spooning.

I Remember What She Said

Cry damn it.
Go ahead, it's not going to change anything.
Cry like a little girl
That's all little-girls do is cry,
And lie

Cry for 'me' damn it
Show me how much you regret it.
Sissies cry and that's what you are
So sorry, so sad, so pathetic
And weak

Cry loud damn it
I know you want to. I can see it.
Turn on the water works.
Not big enough to stand up for yourself
Or run

I said cry G'D damn it
It's the only thing you no how to do
Sit there impotent
Do nothing at all but cry
Like me
Cry G'D damn you, because I do want to be... alone

A Dozen Thoughts

Every day I write a half dozen letters to you.

Have three times as many conversations still.

Words are never inscribed on a page,
banged out on a keyboard or resonated in your ears.

The words are housed, cradle to crave, among the swirling
in my head.

Every day I remember the half dozen letters you wrote to
me.
Sentiments, questions, and answers that could be
exchanged if we continued.

It's comforting to remember your smile and apply it to
newly imagined interactions.

Conversations we have and plans we make- each perfect;
not hindered with reality.

Every day I only write these words to you, so few are ever
spoken.

The words are true and remain benign in every way, safely
anchored on the page.

Internal smiles bloom in me like tulips providing reservoirs
to receive more of you.

I write, imagining everything as I want it to be at any given
moment, and it pleases you.

Every day you read only a few words from me, and I am overjoyed.

Where I Go when I am Not with You

Often, I do the same thing. Sleep the time away.
I often just roll my eyes...
Into the back of my head, and fade away

Often, I just shut my mind too. Fast forwarding through
the slow parts.
I often simply wander away from my body...
Choosing to live in my fantasy while my reality fails to start.

Often, I just set back and forget myself. Hiding as I do.
I often do nothing, simply nothing at all....
Playing in the memories of you.

My Favorite

My favorite things to do is to lay down with you,
Too have upon my chest the weight of your breast.
Feeling you resting into oblivion.
Cares faded and worries abated
One of my favorite things to do is to lay down with you

My favorite thing to do is to tell you of my day.
Give you my daily report and hear your boisterous retort.
Your opinion sensitively lay before me.
Words carefully chosen and my heartbeat still and frozen.
One of my favorite things to do is to tell you of my day.

My favorite thing to do is to hold you in my arms.
Squeezing you tight, feeling that in a world of wrong, this, I
know is right.
Our bodies exchanging heat to a level calm.
My arms against you pressed, the feel of my strength allows
you to rest.
One of my favorite things to do is to hold you in my arms.

My favorite thing to do is to think of you loving me.
Placing your heart on the line with only faith, I will return it
to you in kind.

You know love is dangerous, yet you brave it with me still.
Nothing hidden, all exposed, you allow your heart to be
rejected or chosen.
One of my favorite things is to do is think of you loving me.

My favorite thing to do is to feel how I feel with you next to
me.
You far away, a shallow pain, and your love in my heart an
eternal refrain.
Each touch is pleasant so far, if you're to leave it would be a
pleasant scar.
With careless passion we did burn, ever brighter with each
season turned.
One of my favorite things to do is to feel how I feel with you
next to me.

My favorite thing to do is to...
Know how you feel next to me and think of you loving me.
Hold you in my arms.
Tell you of my day as down with you I lay.
My favorite thing to do, is in all these ways be in love with
you.

My Weakness for Her

There is a firmness inside me
and outside of me.
Craving.

To be the man inside of you
in your softer thoughts.
Pressing.

Atop of you on your pedestal
and beneath you.
Resting.

Beside you in a waking dream
in your wildest reality.
Pushing.

Against you, through you, deeper
and within you.
Holding.

Myself back from my needs
in quiet panic waiting.
Plunging

My Weakness for Her Continued...

Deeper into you my thoughts pry
and embody you.
Banging.

My Weakness for Her Continued...

Like a drunken college freshman
in a rented room.
I Do
Do, You.

All This Time

We all have those late nights.
Those nights when there is no reason for us to be awake.
Inspiration, for once is not a no-show.
And we find our great ideas and elaborate mistakes.

We all have those late nights.
Those nights that precede a darker day to come.
The clocks buzzing loudly, projecting time in LCD.
Like deer staring at its light, not frightened but stunned.

We all have those late nights.
Those nights when we catch up on our mental production of crap.
Processing in great mass with minimal production.
Praying once out of our system the streak will snap.

We all have those late nights.
Those late nights with no explanation forth coming.
Planted there, occupying pace and being drain time.
Too tired to sleep, we watch the clock tic on, forever-running.

Sculpting Recollections

Waking moments are more than a realization of what's in front of you, who is with you or who has you in their grasp.

Waking moments are those times we carve into memories. Times when we part the waters of life, as opposed to being tossed about under the crushing tides of the unexpected.

Waking moments are those times we take control of how out of control we want to be and with whom and for what. Knowing that looking back will bring almost as much pleasure as looking forward.

Waking moments don't come to us spontaneously, we make them. Call them front and center as if we are generals leading a great- army. Preparing to conquer the fates and scorching our chosen way ahead.

Waking moments are the times I lay awake thinking of you naked at the precise moment you have chosen to comply with my request.

Waking moments are the moments when I drift off thinking of you. Fall asleep dreaming of us together, and awake consumed with thoughts of you compelled to give you more of me.

What Do I Say?

What do I say to you now?
Now that you are listening.
Now that you care.

What do I say to you now?
Now that you've heard my truths.
Now that you understand.

What do I say to you now?
Now that that you've heard my lies.
Now that you like those words.

What do I say to you now?
Now that you are tired of listening.
Now that you have heard it all before.

What do I say to you now?
Now that the lies sound better than the truth.
Now that you're listening to your inner voice.

What do I say to you now?
Now that my words fall on deaf ears.
Now that you are making decisions without me.

What do I say to you now?
Now that decisions are made.
Now that what I say no longer matters.

It's All Good.

The nights are good when I let my mind drift.
Drift freely to think of what feels best.
That makes me happy.

The mornings are good when I let my mind wander,
Wander foolishly into sleep the night before.
 That makes me happy.

Good mornings and nights born of the same thoughts.
When I let my mind wander, it returns to you.
This makes me happy.

Dancing

A giggle, a jump, a shake.
A shimmy, a saunter, a wiggle.
A wobble, a whirl, a Twerk!
A Tengo, a waltz, a Polka!
A Hoedown... Get down... Boogie...

Let's go Dancing!

Your Love or Mine?

Your love is like rain-
    it washes over me,
    nourishes me,
    drowns me,
    and it ends too soon.
Your love is like a canopy of trees-
    it shelters me,
    shades me,
    obscures me,
    and consumes me.
Your love is like sunlight-
    bathing me in warmth,
    illuminating my path forward,
    and blinding me from danger.
Your love is like my imagination-
    it is perfectly ideal,
    exactly portioned,
    and overwhelming plentiful,
Your love is like my love-
    it frightens me and I crave more.

One Way to Do It

All of our lives are built on lies
They are the lies we tell ourselves
But they are the lies we choose to believe.

Believing is what gives us hope.
Believing the lies is what gets us through
Believing is not easy, we commit to the work.

Though we each knows great deal
The sum of which is too heavy to know it
These lies we need, compressed under their weight into
faith.

Faith is a beautiful thing
Forbearance for our own lies in our hearts
Fraught by the truth with faith we can hold on to our lies.

We lie to ourselves
We live with ourselves and these lies,
We believe the lies we tell, and the ones we live.

I'm Sorry

Forgiveness is a difficult task.
Best leave it for God.
From that, you know me.

And the volume of hate I carry in my heart.

Hard Truth

No one has ever lied to me as often as I have lied to myself.

Simple Truth

Just lie to the kids.
They will never know.
They will never now until it's time to lie to their kids.

Not My Truth

If we hope to end Evil,
We first must first police Evil.
In ourselves.
Each and every one of us.

The Weapon Truth

Knowledge of the truth is sharp blade that never dulls.
A tool that never wears.
A weapon without equal.
Making victims of both the attacked and the wielder.

Food and Prey

I breath in your pain.
I exhale my love for you.
You inhale my love for you.

You send more pain.
Keeping the engine running.
I live for you, inhaling, exhaling.

I kill myself for you.
Exhaling my life to you.
Breathing in your pain.

Same World Different Planet

We walk through this world.
Our minds tied behind my back.
Shackled by reflex emotions.
Responding to what we think others feel.

FODEC

If you are to choose the light,
you must first face the darkness.

If you are to walk in the light,
You must defend against the night.

If you choose the darkness,
The righteous may show no mercy.

Walking in darkness, you must defend against the light.
You will also need to defend against others who have also
chosen darkness.

"My" Bad

I could pave a road across the seven seas.
Pave a road using the opportunities I have wasted.

When I look back there is no guilt, or regent in my wake.
This is because they were my opportunities to waste.

The Greatest Goods

Perhaps the best contribution you can make to the world is to take proper care of your home and your family.

But to do this means nothing if you do not consider the earth your home, and its inhabitants your family.

A Vision of Life in Death

I saw a dead man yesterday.
It was his funeral.

I saw a dead man yesterday.
Heard the wailing of his children.
Tears filled the eyes of his grandchildren.

I saw a dead man yesterday.
Surrounded by his friends-60, 70, 80 even 90 years old.
Hunched over, beaten, gnarled.

I saw a dead man yesterday.
A good man whose death brought many to say good-bye.
Mourners lay their hands on his weathered skin,

I saw a dead man yesterday...at a funeral.
I saw a dead man yesterday and for the first time saw peace.
Though I cherish life, and savor each moment lived.

I saw a dead man yesterday and felt true envy.

Related Thoughts

It is human nature to strive;
To struggle against.

And when there is nothing left to struggle against.
We struggle against ourselves.

+   +   +

There are many paths in life.
In fact, there are many true paths.

But there may be only one path that holds true to you.

+   +   +

At times, the price of the greater good is to great.

Self-Preservation

Occasionally, I feel broken.
Limping through the tasks in my day, hoping no one
notices.

I wake up and say, good morning worries.
Worries greets my guilt and asks after my obsessions, which
have had no rest.

Standing apart from myself.
Wielding a piercing objectivity, judging me when no one
does.

Overactive in my sense of responsibility.
There are no causes of suffering or greatness but me.

Others are toiling toward the greater good.
Working tirelessly, so long as the greater good points
toward their own agenda.

It makes sense then to rely only on myself.
Expecting nothing from others without exception,
preventing disappointment.

How Fighting Continues

There are those of us struggling.
Struggling to hold the darkness at bay.

But this is not enough.
Enough to keep the darkness from over taking the light.

We must use our light to ignite others to shine.
Shine, and hold the darkness at bay when we are gone.

Salutations

Good morning Guilt!
Good morning Worries!
Have you seen Obsession this morning?
No, I am afraid obsession may have stayed up all night
again.

Images from Life as I Imagine Them

I Don't Want to Stop

I just had a chat that lasted about an hour and the conversation was driven mostly by how I think of myself and my regard you. You are so down to earth and, in some ways, completely unreachable; it is a good balance I suppose. It was the best conversations had this week.

Although I never mentioned you, I thought of you as I put my thoughts together. Mostly I thought of how authentic you are, true to yourself without apology. How you are able to mean what you say, protect yourself, but also be open to helping others.

This was the longest conversation I have had outside of a meeting in weeks. When was the last time you had a long meandering conversation that made you smile to yourself, laugh inside, or glower with introspection? Even though I asked these questions I don't expect responses- but I would love to hear your answers. Still not expect anything but bubbling with hopes. Hopes that you smile, laugh and dance. Hope that you still find things that surprise you, move you to tears, and provide you with fodder to tell tall tales to old friends and whopping lies to strangers.

My chat today was about Living. Living an authentic life, being true to myself and still living safely. How to live, and grab those extraordinary highs that life has to offer and keep from crumbling to pieces should I fall from those heights. The conversation was rewarding, because of how I have heard you speak of the mundane as if it were the supernatural and give rise to the thoughts of fantastic dreams that could be made true with small deliberate actions; everything so clear, simple. Our conversations were models for how to speak my mind.

Why was I thinking about you during this chat??? Because it made me happy to do so, and conversations are better with you in them.

Grow Up!

Less than five feet tall wasn't low enough to stay off her radar as a little girl; clambering beneath her feet. OOP!!!! Pick me! Pick Me! Love me! I have an Idea!

Calm down, sit down, be quiet, and grow up.

Passing the time was being passed off, passed over and passed around.

What do you want to be? Who do you want to be like?

Be more like a lady, you're just like your mom! Go ask your brother...

Complemented through condescension, interested only in my lack of interest, and raised having each downfall highlighted. I'll show her. When I get older, when I am a big girl, when I make my own decisions. When I grow up.

You don't know... You're too small... You're too young... You couldn't possibly understand!!!

I'll tell you when you're older. Then you'll understand, when you're all grown up.

Well, I am older now mom. My own woman now mom, and I do understand. I know why you never listened. And I understand all those things your never told me. I know why you would never explain. It's been over thirty years since I left, and I know
now what you knew then...You didn't know shit! And you were scared... and if you and I are anything alike mother,

then chances are you were ashamed. But don't worry
mother, my daughter won't find out until she grows up.

The Road from Here to Her

The space between you and I is no great chasm or void.
Not the Royal Gorge or ring of fire it wishes us to believe. The
Space between you and I is powerless but without fear. The
space between you and I is undersized for the job it has taken.
Too weak to be of any concern anymore. The space cowers in the
shadow of our endurance. The space between you and I, it huffs
and puffs at the beginning of each day thrashing around violently,
sporadically. The space between you and I is beginning to notice
that we no longer flinch at its bluffs, we no longer quiver in our
hearts and stand frozen in fear. The Space between you and I is
angry and spites us with sixty hate full breaths a minute. The
space is growing tired and knows that though it may wrap itself
around us it can never crush us. The space had planned to erode
our spirits away. That is the way of the space. The Space
between us has a name that is spelled with no capital letters or
other bold punctuations. The space between us is growing
smaller. The space between us is dying. And when we are
together, we will love, we will laugh, and we will Live, again.

I am with You Now

Sitting here in the dark basking in the light that are thoughts of you. Sunday is not just another day to get through; Sunday is a day that I like to think of as ours. That brief 24 hour period before it is time to go to work again. That short time when without guilt I am able to enjoy the very thing I am working for...Us.

Sundays are for us to lay still. The day can be rainy, slow and quiet; it's not the weather that makes the day. These still moments makeup my favorite days. I like nothing so much as to hear you take in those shallow inhalations under my chin. As your head rises and falls on my chest, I breath in your tiny breaths. Feeling your body absorb my heat like a spark arching from a doorknob to your hand.

Sitting in Sunday silence. Sitting and nearly asleep, too comfortable to do anything at all. Tap, tap, tap on the window raindrops fall playing natures' symphony. Sundays when we fall asleep together midday and awake in each other's arms. Same position as when we started.

Too comfortable to do anything turns to a physical expression of love and pleasure. Sunday, the day I awake twice in your arms. Sunday, the day when the only energy I spend is on you. Hands through your hair, my cheek against your neck with lips grazing your neck. Sunday, the day when personal space is defined as that tangle of legs and pelvis that is done shamelessly with the lights on.

Sunday is the day we have time to experience ourselves. Today is the day when my hands feel strong, your skin extra smooth and your flesh receptive. Today is the day when my grip around your waste isn't just an invitation but a demand grown from my daily fantasies and your silent pleas.

Sunday, today, the day when the couch is our gymnasium and the workout is hard presses, leaving our muscles soar and shaky. Today is the day when everything fades into one beautiful color and we see each other's body through our eyelids. Heads swaying backwards and from side to side.

Today is a day when our lips lock, hearts meld together and we explore each other with fingertips and tongues. My left-hand glides, across your hip and onto your backside taking more time than necessary to get where you prefer it. Today is a day when the convention is forgotten, and the potion of passion is mixed with two parts love and generous helping of lust. Today is the day when me being a hard man is more than a description of my personality, it's a physical reality that you create. A reality that you control, a reality that has no other purpose than to pleasure you.

Today is a day when getting dressed in the morning is a formality that neither of us takes seriously. A pair of boxers for me and for you my oversized Lafayette shirt that barley covers your comfortable fitting panties. Sunday, today, is the day when I fall out of my boxers on a more than regular bases. The day when the extra-large armhole in your shirt welcomes my hands to your breast and breakfast is postponed because we need the counter space for ourselves. Today is Sunday. It is slipping by too fast and I too slowly into you. Out of you. In you further still. Today is Sunday, our day, and I am with you now.

Strange Bed Fellows

This weekend has been a long one. Now that it is over, however, I can hardy remember it save for this. I went to Christi's", from the club's birthday party. I learned a lot about her and her husband but nothing that bears repeating. Esmerelda the Bartender and her husband showed up. They invited me to dinner. They are not the types of people with whom I think I should align myself. Both of them talk about things they shouldn't in front of people they hardly know. Also, I spent Friday evening with the Beverly's. They always have fun stories to listen too. But at the end of both evenings, I was left empty.

My mother called and tried to tell me how to take care of the cat and that you would be returning soon. I snapped at her and told her to be quiet. Until then, I did not realize that I missed you so. I am so sick of everyone telling me that you'll be home soon, and that time will fly by. To that I say, Bullshit! I know that you won't be back for quite a long time and what is worse- talking about it just makes me think about the time without you all the more. I am lonely, yes but it is so much more than that. I feel as if I have a broken arm. My life with you requires me to use parts of me mentally, emotionally and physically that I cannot when you are gone. I know you love me and that is what carries me most days. I don't, however, need anyone else asking me how you are doing. Because the truth is, I don't know.

I know what you tell me, but I can't feel what you feel like at home. My heartbeat has nothing to keep time with when I fall asleep. --There is so much that weighs down on me every day and without you here to distract me I noticed every waking moment. Most recently I have begun to dream about it as well- and the space between you and me.

I have done so many things lately that I know I should enjoy but the experiences always seem somehow deflated. My laughter trails off into the silence of an empty room and I listen to it falter. I feel my smile fade and cheeks soften into sadness because there is no harmony in my solo laugh.

I worry about so much. Little things that I know you enjoy. I do everything I can to keep the echoes of your presence from fading away from the apartment. I try to silence the voice in my head that screams in pain for your return. I hear those fading reverberations and drift into an imaginary world where you and I laugh together, smile together, and hold each other; closing out the rest of the world, protected by a tower of love tempered in passion, and sealed with sincerity.

I have not spoken so much about "I" in such a very long time. Without you here it is so easy to reflect upon myself and see the imperfections. I know that I have something inside me which you love so very much. Something inside that is good and true, but it is locked away awaiting your return. All I can do to try and tolerate myself while you are gone, make myself look and feel better about who I am without you, but not change who it is you love.

I am not depressed; I am only disappointed. Disappointed in the cruel fact of life, that sacrifice of this kind must be made. That I must give up a piece of us as well as myself in the hope that something more will be returned to us in the future.

*   *   *

I woke up early today. Not early-early. But it early enough to do what I needed done. I donned my workout clothes. Tightly laced my shoes. Comfy shoes. Well Worn into the shape of my feet. I descended slowly down the stairs. Hearing the symphony of creaking and cracking. The stairs and my bones. The front door of the house is heavy. My feet felt just as heavy. Dragging. My Feet and my ass through the foyer. Darkness enfolds me so I return to flip on the porch light. To kindle and stoke my motivation, I look into the brightness. After unlocking the car door, I land plump into my seat. Inhale, cough, exhale and repeat. Repeat. Start the engine. Repeat. My muscles scream in sore resistance as I turn the wheel to exit the drive. On my way now; to the best part of my day. On my way now. It hurts so much. On my way now. There now. Time to go in now. I want to stay

Swenson's Last Ride

He sat there like he had before in so many strip clubs; his hands wrapped around behind the small of his back- a true gentleman. The
light in the room was provided by a half dozen, hand sculpted, Perigold coral candles. The fluttering illumination danced across his face and glints reflected from his Rolex pockmarked the walls and ceiling. Seated, reclining really, on the black Club Deep 96" leather sofa, he was panting and sweating through his custom cut shirt and black Armani suit jacket; the collar around his burgundy Ermenegildo tie had become damp and tightened around his neck.

Eyes closed, mouth agape with lips tremoring, he was distracted by the sharp nagging pain in his left temple. The more he moved his head the worse the pain. So, he relented and sat motionless as she hitched up her black Dolce & Gabbana mini dress with sterling silver gromets leading from her left thigh upwards across her center line, below the deep V-neck butterfly collar, and upward to the single flat-braided shoulder strap of her outstretched right arm.

She settled into the cadence of the music, *Easy* by The DaniLeigh & Chris Brown remix, thumping through a set of twelve-inch retro Cerwin Vegas speakers. She began with a slow twerking grind from his kneecap lengthwise along his over-developed quadricep until her right knee crashed into his testicles. He flinched. The pain at the side of his left temple intensified.

"Focus", he told himself in a gasping whisper so low even he couldn't hear it over the music.

Now she felt certain she was enjoying herself more than he. His pulse quickened and so did hers. When she retreated down back to his kneecap, lightly grazing her labia down his leg, she could feel him tremble. It aroused her in a way that was expected. So, she continued for through to the end of the song and a few minutes into the next. She had taken great care of herself physically over the years- could do this for hours if that's what she chose.

She had run track in high school and college; the one hundred, two hundred and anchor for the four by one hundred relays. Fitness was her religion. Her body remained a reflection her commitment. Both breasts still sat high and full; sides pressed and spilling slightly over both sides of the deep V. Their curves sweeping symmetrically like small navel oranges. They moved harmoniously exactly two large thumb widths apart. The V-neck outlined a sexual promenade leading upwards to angelic-beauty and downward to devilish-satisfaction.

The dress she wore was like a second skin and left no room for undergarments or imagination. A polyamide spandex blend, the dress held close to her skin but also allowed her to feel the natural motion of her body as she lurched back and forth. She loved the way she felt in this dress; looked in this dress, and it pissed her off that he wasn't watching.

Using her left hand, she grabbed a fist full of his product filled salt-n-peppered hair. The lush locks were styled, not cut, and were a useful tool used in grabbing his undivided attention. Squeezing both sides of his head tightly, she arched her back and smashed her sternum into his nose- his eyes closed again. He could taste the sweat now beading up on her chest. The smell of her custom mix of Channel No. 5 and Chance invaded through his nostrils to set up camp at the roof of his mouth. He didn't dare stick out his tongue taste her warm tanned skin. He knew she would see this as rude, and small part of him thought if he played his cards right, this could end with a bang.

His tremors and trembles became more apparent, and she, more aroused- aggressive. Clamping her legs together as tightly as possible, trapping his limp member between her knee and his groin she escalated; knowing that as she raked her breasts across his wilting lips, she was making it difficult for him to breath. She knew because her sternum began to ache hard-pressed against the bridge of his nose. She felt the heat from the sweat rolling down from his brow. Reveling in this moment of power and control was bringing her to climax. She felt a devious pleasure in the thought of leaving a completely obvious stretch of her ecstasy along the length of his pant-leg. Grinding and groaning, she smiled wide showing the flawless work Dr. Margueles, Hollywood's best cosmetic dental surgeon.

At last, she released her self-restraint, let herself flow a deluge that poured like water from a faucet. She felt the warm stream down around her calf, across her ankle and into her Louboutin Privet Patent Red Sole stiletto pumps with the black lacquer bows. As she shuddered and pumped, the last of her joy soaking through his pants and on to his skin, he remained motionless. Except for his trembling jaw- it hadn't slowed beat. His eyes remained closed, arms going numb behind his back, and his plump lips quivered- slightly parted.

"Did you like that baby", she asked lustfully into the ear opposite his temple's pain.

Not waiting for him to answer, she pulled a folded four-inch square paper from an artfully hidden pocket from the small of the back of favorite her dress. Shoved it between is slack lips and pulled the trigger. The right side of his head burst like giant pimple, leaving remnants on the Basquiat painting across the room.

The painting was, like everything else they owned together, expensive. An acrimonious gift from his parents for their 11th anniversary last year. She huffed at the sight of the ruined painting.

Then, without ceremony, she climbed onto the sofa. The stiletto-heal on her left foot gave way awkwardly as it poked a hole through the upholstery. After gathering her dress to above her hips, she straddled his well-dressed lifeless body and relieved herself. It was such a sweet relief she felt. Like when she finally arrived home from that god-awful marathon drive from the Grand Canyon with her parents, summer of her sophomore year in high school.

    Taking care to pat herself dry using his tie, she looked down and could see the cost on the hospital invoice she had shoved into his mouth a few minutes earlier. The number read, Seventeen-thousand, five-hundred eighty dollars, and fifty-two cents. This final invoice, a shattered eye socket, wired jaw, and two dental surgeries is was what this dance cost her. This Danza de la Libertad.

    After dismounting, careful not to trip herself on the heal she caught in the sofa during her ascension, she slid her dress back into place, donned her tan Burberry raincoat, pulled her tangled curls from between her back, and the coat's collar, and

then fluffed her hair into what can only be described as a state of glamor. She casually toppled over one the lighted coral candles next to the Tiffany drapes, as she made her way for the exit. Instantly, the room was illuminated so bright she was forced to squint.

    The stride of pride to the mahogany wood trimmed threshold was longer than she expected- she could feel the oppressive heat build behind her. When her eyes fully adjusted to the light on her way out of the living area, into the foyer, she caught a glimpse of her own smile in a brass trimmed mirror at the end of the hall. She continued on without breaking stride, passed the redwood roundtable where her former husband's wedding band lay- finger still inside. Pausing briefly at the door, setting it to lock automatically behind her, she walked out of the three-story, 5-bedroom 5-bath, colonial with in-ground kidney bean-pool for the last time.

This Doesn't End with Hello

One of the first intimate things she learned about him was that he like to write. That is to say, expressing himself in written form brought him pleasure- he is an emotional exhibitionist putting all out there to see, unapologetically.

During the moment he divulged this personal truth, cocktail glasses clanked, and royals of laughter bellowed throughout the room; she heard none of it. Later she'll recall thinking, "this is a benign piece of information, likely a lie to appear interesting. A tidbitof small talk used to sway my decision." But it was actually an unsubtle truth signaling an openness she hadn't expected.

Flaxen hair, cut sharply punk but styled with the care of a more sophisticated woman, framed her face. Her smooth ceramic skin boasted the firmness of young co-Ed. And when she laughed, small plump lips, painted with a clearly high-end cosmetic, parted to reveal a slightly crooked smile. The smile was coy, and to him, savagely erotic.

Although he outwardly appeared as confident as he was tall, occasionally, when she smiled, a nervousness crept into his voice. When he spoke, he stared deeply into the twin blue sapphires that were her eyes, which were fearless and openly challenged him to keep her attention. And it was when she allowed her eyes to break his gaze she found his gaze was not what had her attention.

His shoulders were broad but not angular,
biceps thick- forearms vascular and wrapped in caramel-
skin supple like the young college athletes she was
accustomed to dating. But the folds that appeared in his
face when he grinned accented a distinguished although
not overstated jaw line of a middle-aged man, a welcome
change from the bulk of her recent suitors. And when she
made him laugh, his smile flashed without modesty.

In these beginning moments- standing, talking,
walking, laughing, and washing each other with their eyes.
Each in their own time became alerted by the hummingbird
beats in their respective chests that they were again
hunters!
Hunters, who were now being hunted.

"Keys, Wallet, Phone"

Tweet, whistle-whistle, tweet.

"Fucking birds!"

Jāzley grumbled angrily, pulling the pillow over her head and kicking her left leg from under the heavy Martha Stewart Elite comforter to equalize her temperature.

Tweet, whistle-whistle, tweet.

"FuckiNG BIRDS!" this time groaning the words through her teeth more loudly, tossing the pillow to the ground and then opening her eyes for the first time about 2am that morning. Staring upward at the ceiling, she could see sun rays falling through the hall from the living room window into her bedroom; ultimately streaking against the yellow blackout curtains blocking the bedroom's south wall windows- "how pretty she thought"

"Shit!" the word barreled out of her cottoned mouth like buck shot from a shot gun. Casting the bedding aside with disgust she stumbled off the California-King Tempur-pedic. Traversing the high pile cream white carpet into the master bathroom and directly into the shower without closing the cloth no-ring curtain or waiting for it to warm.

Water droplets stabbed at her; bouncing off of youthfully buoyant skin, soaking the floor and bathmat adjacent to the tub. The cool water forced her into a state of alertness. A few pumps a body wash into her left hand and the waterproof Oral-B in her right. Hurriedly smearing the wash across areas, she deemed essential following a night out, and scrubbing her teeth like a polygraph needle attached to a presidential candidate. Without thinking she lowered her head under the three mode Speakman square head.

"Fuck!"

She didn't want to waste time with washing her hair, and the subsequent styling regimen. So she used both hands to wring the bulk of water from her hair, then spun the valve control until the flow of water choked to a halt.

Poorly rinsed, soapsuds still bubbling down the length of her spine and collecting in the sculpted small of her back; she stepped out of the shower. One foot on the bathmat the other on cool, wet tile. As she crossed the small well-appointed room to secure the towel left in a garble on the round-raised sink basin, she flexed her toes and quickly scanned her reflection in the studio-lighted mirror. She snatched it up with a snap, then dragged the medium weight Terri-cloth across her skin; scantily drying her anterior and almost

completely neglecting her back. With both hands she guided her wavy blonde hair away from her face, behind lose lobe ears; each freckled with nearly half-a-dozen piercings. Hair secure, turning her attention back toward the master bedroom, she darted beyond the threshold out of the bathroom, and let the towel fall to the floor in a sodden heap.

Before clearing the vanity area adjacent to the bathroom, she fished out three rings from Spanish clay bowl on the counter of the vanity; placed one on her thumb, index and ring fingers of her left hand. On her thumb she placed a square cut translucent orange topaz held by a sterling silver claw. To adorn the index finger, a princess cut, single carrot, flawless diamond set in platinum. Lastly, on the ring finger she slipped on a one and a quarter inch chrome finger cuff sporting a raised relief in the shape of the Eye-of-Ra.

Form the night stand she grabbed a hand full of sterling silver and leather bangles and secured them on her left wrist. Leaving damp footprints behind, she made her way over to the chest of drawers between the two south wall windows. From the top she pulled out a pair of stark white, bikini strap panties and a red Garden Fairy Triangle bra. Cursing all the while

"Shit, shit, shit!" she chanted while pouring herself inside the

brassiere:
hand-elbow- shoulder-breast, repeat. At some point dropping the panties from her left hand and not noticing. Her top secure, she sped off down the hall toward the kitchen and living areas.

Emerging from the corridor she paused for a moment, taken aback by the view through the living room's window. The sun was cresting the mix of pine, maple and oaks that lined the horizon. A bright yellow backsplash silhouetting the treetops giving the illusion of a small mountain landscape. She had intended to be awake before dawn and was no rushing, but she took a moment to cherish the view before her.

Not realizing time was slipping away, looking around at the state of disarray in her kitchen: half eaten gummy bears, dirty shot glasses and a three quarters empty bottle of tequila she didn't remember buying. She thought,

"Last night really got away from me?!"

Her inner voice again in retort,

"Maybe I got away with last night?"

Snapped back into the moment by the changing incline of the sun, which was now washing the trees in gold and strangling her pupils. She lunged forward, back at full pace, hoisting from the dining table-chair a retro 80's, silver semi-sequin club blouse with three quarter-sleeves and extra-large neck-hole. It floated down along the length of her slender fingers and toned arms. Emerging from the bottom of the sleeves, nails painted with a jet-black powder coat.

The bottom of the blouse grazed along her waist and gathered at her hips. The top settled with a snap on her right shoulder just below her still wet hair. The neck-hole, too wide to lay in a traditional manner, slumped three inches below the round of left shoulder exposing the upper portion of a life-long athlete's bicep, the crimson strap of the Fairy Triangle Bra, and an elegantly angled clavicle.

When her head emerge through the top of the blouse, she opened her eyes and saw she was facing the refrigerator. Large, but perfectly sized for the Tuscan styled kitchen, the unit was configured with French doors above two drawers: a quick access snack drawer with a hidden slot handle at her navels' height. Six inches below, a matching handle slot used to roll out the two-tier freezer compartment.

Brilliant blue numbers beaming from the center of the left French door read 07:13am. The fridge compressor kicked on, sputtered. She sighed and her stomach growled. As she stepped toward the fridge, she remembered catching a glimpse of her abdomen and waistline in the vanity mirror when stepping out from the shower. She liked what she saw. She had even smirked at herself at the time. With echoes of this positive self-image resurging in her mind, she abruptly changed course and grabbed an organic meal replacement bar from the silver toped glass jar on the quartz counter-top adjacent to the fridge's matching gas range. Tore open the pink and yellow reflective cellophane wrapper, took a bite too large to chew, and tossed the remainder into a bowl in the sink containing two spoons and the soupy remnants of leftover pralines and cream.

More determined than ever, scowling through a pair of chipmunk cheeks, she shuttled from the kitchen, to master bedroom and then on into the master bath searching for her favorite black stretch jeans with the decorative slashes on the thighs. Failing to find them in either place she redirected her hunt down the hall where saw a sock, half turned inside out, and found her memory.

Upon her return home the late the night before she immediately began shedding clothes at the door's threshold. Peeling off her Lady Harley leather scooter jacket that sported zippers on the wrist and neck cuffs. A quilted pad above the left breast pocket- wrapping over, then around the scapula. Using the ball of her left foot she easily scraped the heal of her custom order low-top Chuck Taylor from her right foot. The low-rise booty sock remained in the shoe when she stepped forward. Hands and attention more focused elsewhere, attempting the same maneuver with the opposite foot, the left shoe protested until she kicked, and it released across the living room; landing in some dark corner with a thwack.

Jeans unbuttoned, zipper retracted, attempting to roll them away from her skin- damp with perspiration. Stepping with a high knee down the hall, the right foot was extricated with ease. The left foot, still inside the sock's cotton sleeve resisted. In a fit of frustration, she stamped down the right pant leg, already on the floor, while bringing the left knee as high as she could without falling over or losing her grip. With a snap, the left foot was free. The left pant leg wrapping around the right ankle and the sock bounding down the hall, careening off the walls and coming to rest just short of the kitchen tile. She kicked again with her right leg again and she was free.

Replaying the events in her mind, warm and goose fleshed from the memory, she ambled with a quickness to the guess bathroom off the hall. Entering the darkened room with eyes wide, she toggled the switch to on. Now squinting from the bright light, she snatched up her quarry which lay splayed inside out; one leg draped over the tub sill and the other across the bathmat and next to the toilet.

Her smart watch sounded with a blink as she glided the pant leg up the curves of her right calf and quad. Her candy apple red toes budding out of the other end like flowers peddles after springs first rain. Not taking the time to button or zip, she used her left hand to fold the blouse over the open pants, and the right hand to pull back her hair as she raced into the living room to find her shoes.

The smart watch continued to glow and ping as she put on her right shoe and searched for the left. The do not disturb setting on the smartwatch was no longer enabled.

"Shit!" she says again, audibly. Because she knew the repeated chimes and vibrations meant that it had to be 7:30. The goal was to be gone by 7am.

While frantically scrambling around the living area she catches the reflection of her left shoe in a side wall mirror. The sound from last night was the shoe lodging itself between the flat screen television and the wall on which it was mounted. After fishing it from behind the monitor by the shoestring, she made her way over to the main seating area and rested against the arm of the sofa. While choking down the last of the oversized mouthful of the organic meal replacement bar, and her foot falls into the left custom Chuck with a thud.

With an exasperated inhale and exhale she erects herself, slips into the scooter jacket flung on to the sofa cushions the previous night and begins checking the pockets.

"Keys, wallet, phone... Shit!"

All the pockets are empty. Gliding her palms around her rump pockets she discovers her phone in left pocket. Removes it and thumbs the right-side button to illuminate the screen.

"7:33am | 17% Battery"

"Fuck!" Jāzley blurts in a huff, "I'll charge it in the car."

Whirling around from the sofa to commence the hunt for the remaining necessary items her toes, now comfortably wrapped in the Converse Allstar shoes died to match the blouse she was now wearing, nudge something on the floor. It's her wallet. Using her left hand to guide her decent, kneeling down like a southern debutant, she scooped up the Spanish leather wallet adorned with tassels. And jammed into her right jacket pocket.

"Fuck yeah...Bitches! Now where are my God..."

Before she can finish her sentence, she has another spontaneous recollection, or rather a realization her memory was incomplete. She remembered putting the key in the door lock when arriving home but didn't remember closing the door behind her or the signature sound of the keys slamming down and skidding along the Arhaus driftwood coffee table.

Exhaling a nervous groan and wearing wince that nearly closes her left eye, she turns the antique, 1930s pewter knob she installed last winter and slowly opens the front door.

The keys are there, sparkling in the bath of morning sunrays. The house key lingering in the lock case like a frat boy spooning his girlfriend after drunken romp.

"Fuck yeah!" she exclaims, loud enough to spook the birds gathered three floors below in the parking lot.

The sun is completely above the tree-line now and the cool of the night is starting to give way to the warmth of the coming day. Bursting through the breezeway, clambering down the external concrete stairway, skipping as many steps as the length of her legs would allow, she catches the eye of Mr. Harmless with her own.

Mr. Harmless was how she referred to the guy across the courtyard in 2B who was always standing in his robe staring out the window and waved at anyone who came along. She pitied him, although she did understand fully why. She, however, was always sure to wave on her way out. He was kind enough in turn to never approach her or ask for more than this simple gesture. Attempting to keep the tradition she nearly lost her balance descending the last three stairs onto the surface lot. She recovered quickly, waved. Then broke into a run.

Not at full sprint, her car was too close to warrant that, but run none the less. It was fewer than five second before she reached the door of her John Cooper Works edition. It was parked somewhat wonky between the lines, but the front bumper was facing out the way she liked. Unlocking the doors mid run, she was able to immediately fling the driver-side door open and leaped inside the Recaro fashioned driver's seat the moment her hand could grasp the door handle.

She pushed the auto start button and heard the throaty exhaust of the 228hp engine come alive. Placing her left hand on the leather wrapped wheel at the twelve o'clock position, gripped it tightly, then softened her grip enough to rock her wrist into a comfortable position; palm grinding against the stitching. The dash came alive with amber and white lights as she cradled the gear shift in her palm and let out a victorious exhale.

It was 7:43am on Sunday and 80% of businesses were closed because of the virus. She inhaled deeply, slowly. Her shoulders unstiffened. A single bead of sweat rolled down from her temple, along her angled cheek bone, and beneath her chin. The pre-programed driver settings already lowering the window in pace with that cooling single drop of sweet. Bing, Bing, her cell phone sounds as it syncs with the car's tech package. Grasping it from her pocket with her right hand, she reset it to Do Not Disturb and dropped it carelessly into the empty cup holder.

One last deep inhale followed by a long exhale and her heartbeat fluttered. A wry smile grew on her face. A final check of the dashboard clock reveals its Sunday, 7:44am. As she releases the clutch and mashes down on the accelerator, screeching out of the lot she lets out a Woohoo! Thinking to herself the roads are empty, the tank is full, and there no crisis for me to fix; life is good!

No sooner was this thought complete, did Jāzley's phone begin buzzing, rattling, and flashing in the cup holder.

Haiku do you do?

Splitting Aces

It's every few years
A feeling comes to the surface
Primes the soul with hope.

It's every few years
We are fueled and give chase.
Empowered, bold, sure.

Our souls full, exposed,
We persist without reason.
Dull swords, paper shields.

Possibilities,
There are only positives
They *are* worth the risk.

It's every few years
Chasing joy to exhaustion
Deplete all reserves

Rare in our lifetime,
Place the all or nothing bet.
Beat the odds and win.

Butterfly

Oh, surprise new love.
This is my ending.
We begin us now.

Choice

Beauty or hunger.
Eyes closed; the mouth opens wide,
But will not eat her.

Consequences

Warm, elated, safe.
Scared, hungry, starving by choice.
Life short, satisfied.

Letting Go

Every day it's you.
Each day I remember you.
Every day it's you.

Holding On

I am an addict.
Pay with my life for desires.
Craving what kills me.

Backing Up

Here I give again.
False hope fueling me to you.
Feels so good, false hope.

Sheople

Who knows what to do?
Someone tell me what to do?
This is all your fault.

Little Bird

Tweet-tweet, Little Bird.
Whoosh, Splash, Wind, Rain, darkness falls
Little Bird come home.

Don-old

I Me I Me I.
I'm Great, The Best, POWERFUL
I AM President

New Life 2020

Masks and rubber gloves
Bandanas, social distance
Misinformation

Laying in Memories of Us

So swollen, it hurts...
Remember us together?
I swell, smile, it hurts.

Selfish-Coward

What I do to live
Doesn't pay for who I wish
To do while living

This Makes No Sense

Always struggling
Looking for a path to peace
Struggling for peace

Heroines and Heroes

Courageous people
Are scared a lot of the time
Scared and move forward

Repetitive Request

Can I burn with you?
Like a Christmas tree campfire.
Down to ash, Repeat!

With Certainty

I will come for you,
Over and over again!
Fill you. Cum for you.

Living Highlights

Inhale, Exhale, Breath.
Life in, life out, without pause
Inhale, Exhale, End.

Authentic

Run by emotions.
Jumping for joy, free, reckless.
Risking the great crash

She was - She is not

You were passionate!
Excited, open, giving...
Truth is, you were drunk.

What to Expect

She will not come back.
She'll never come back you see.
She's moving forward.

Postlude

A Difficult Conversation

Dear Diary,

My wife was very displeased to hear I was writing a *book* and had not shared with her details of my endeavor. Although I explained that I had once shown her a draft copy, of which she gave minimal feedback, she did not seem to recall. She expounded upon her displeasure saying that it was a trigger for her because she hates secrets and lies. (At this point I figured we were no longer only talking about the book).

After several minutes of back and forth, she plainly stated that she felt hurt buy my refusal to share. I felt a flash of indignity at the idea that I could not have something private; something that existed only as I chose. She made her case ardently. In the end, to maintain a civil discourse, I agreed to share some of what was written under the stipulation that she would *not* provide feedback of any kind. My rationale for limiting her from providing feedback was that if I heard her feedback, then I would respond.

"My response could be positive or negative.", I told her.

But whatever the response, it would be initiated by external influence. It would not be simply because I did something I wanted to do, the way I wanted to do it. Trying to convey a better understanding of my point of view I explained...

"I want to write this and have it remained... I want something of me to remain as I wrote it. And if, or when, I am gone people read it and don't like it, who cares. As long as no one reads it, they cannot devalue it or influence it me to make it more like what they want vice who I am. I can hold the, sealed, finished product up high and say, *I did this. There was nothing and then there was this, because I made it so. And it is how it is because chose to be.*

I went on to explain that the moment people don't value a thing it becomes trash. And I could not stomach putting so much of myself into a project just to have it turned into trash by a few offhand comments.

After sharing some of the writings with her, I struggle throughout the remainder of the day to convince myself to keep writing. I really wanted to stop writing. I felt I had lost something in the exchange. I had considered sharing my writing with an acquaintance rather than a loved one so that feedback would have less impact. I did share, and after two days the only feedback I received was, "I have many pieces of thoughts".

So that's it. I should have kept my mouth shut so that I still had something that meant something to me that hadn't been shit on by someone else.

I transcribed the following *"Missing My Man"* from a letter that inspired me to express myself more openly. It was handwritten, in ink. From it I found inspiration to express myself using the words that I had available readily instead of looking for the words that would receive the most accolades in a publishing magazine. It inspired me to express myself for the sake of getting the words out of my heart and head. To take that spaghetti tangle of emotions inside me and comb through them using my words. It inspired me to express myself even if I was missing the right word, or prefect word.

Those imperfect words, the missing words, to me are what most accurately describe the spaghetti of emotions. More accurately, it is the gap- what we cannot express in words- that most aptly expresses the emotions we cannot.

Missing My Man

How I so love you. I will now digress to the topic of you
and I what passion our bodies can create. Our mind
allowed to drift out into what may be the only place that it
can be free.
Oh, I must remember what that is like.

Your writings bring me close. They are so familiar. All that
you write about. I must once again know what it is you
speak of. They remind me of something that seems so far
past, yet I know that it is coming closer by the day. Our
mutual admiration.

Oh, the attraction. Such an intense attraction.

Your kiss. The feel of a roughly shaven face against mine,
moving down, down to my neck, down, down to my breast,
down even further to my stomach.

Oh, how I ache for you. Down, still further.

Oh, how I love you. Your cheeks so rough, so masculine.

We once again have eye contact. I see myself in your
eyes. Can you see your reflection in mine? Keep looking.
You are there.

You have always been there, can you see? We come
together and the passion is undeniable. The love shared
between two people. Incomparable.

I am coming...I am coming home soon.

Land of the Untitled

The night's fashion departs
Through a window, to the street from where I came
Never again at that place will we look.
Upon the sweet face of summers gain

Fathering mass murders by the bunch
We stand proud parents of life's thieves.
Life is a lengthy lonesome wale.
Not caused by us but the fault of T.V.s

There is no id greater than ours
So free from shame we live
Boasting we are mountains,
But we cower and up our post we give.

I climb and claw my way downward
Over others to achieve my gardens acclaim
Muting the voices that lag behind
This shooting star has no ear for pain

Those that follow are but fuel
Using others to pad their feet.
Ladders are carved from spines
From those we call friends also known as weak.

Crashed shut are our minds and eyes
Now no one can catch us from behind.
Our weakness is our competitors' treasure,
A dark secret we hope they cannot find.

There is no end to this
There is no line or summit given to boast.
A moment is not taken to catch our breath
Though eventually we all play failures host.

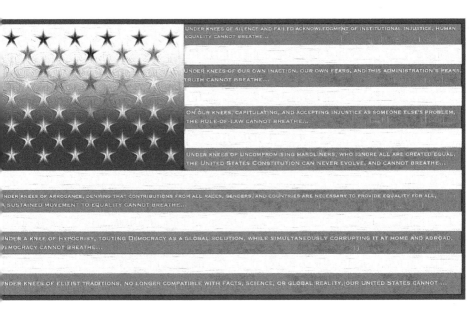

UNDER KNEES OF SILENCE AND FAILED ACKNOWLEDGMENT OF INSTITUTIONAL INJUSTICE, HUMAN EQUALITY CANNOT BREATHE...

UNDER KNEES OF OUR OWN INACTION, OUR OWN FEARS, AND THIS ADMINISTRATION'S FEARS, TRUTH CANNOT BREATHE...

ON OUR KNEES, CAPITULATING, AND ACCEPTING INJUSTICE AS SOMEONE ELSE'S PROBLEM, THE RULE-OF-LAW CANNOT BREATHE...

UNDER KNEES OF UNCOMPROMISING HARDLINERS, WHO IGNORE ALL ARE CREATED EQUAL, THE UNITED STATES CONSTITUTION CAN NEVER EVOLVE, AND CANNOT BREATHE...

UNDER KNEES OF ARROGANCE, DENYING THAT CONTRIBUTIONS FROM ALL RACES, GENDERS, AND COUNTRIES ARE NECESSARY TO PROVIDE EQUALITY FOR ALL, A SUSTAINED MOVEMENT TO EQUALITY CANNOT BREATHE...

UNDER A KNEE OF HYPOCRISY, TOUTING DEMOCRACY AS A GLOBAL SOLUTION, WHILE SIMULTANEOUSLY CORRUPTING IT AT HOME AND ABROAD, DEMOCRACY CANNOT BREATHE...

UNDER KNEES OF ELITIST TRADITIONS, NO LONGER COMPATIBLE WITH FACTS, SCIENCE, OR GLOBAL REALITY, OUR UNITED STATES CANNOT ...

9 781716 876837